SHOLA

AND THE LIONS

SHOLA
AND THE LIONS

Bernardo Atxaga

Illustrated by Mikel Valverde

Translated by Margaret Jull Costa

PUSHKIN CHILDREN'S BOOKS

Pushkin Children's Books
71–75 Shelton Street
London WC2H 9JQ

First published in Euskera (Basque) as
Xolak badu lehoien berri (Erein: 1995)
Translated into Spanish by the author as
Shola y los leones (Ediciones SM: 1995)

This edition published by Pushkin Children's Books in 2015

This English translation is based on the author's Spanish text, and was
first published by Pushkin Children's in 2013 in *The Adventures of Shola*

0 0 1

ISBN 978 1 782690 64 1

Text designed and typeset by Tetragon, London
Printed and bound in China by WKT Co

www.pushkinchildrens.com

SHOLA

AND THE LIONS

One day, Señor Grogó had a visit from a friend who had been travelling round Africa and was longing to tell Grogó about everything he had seen there. Grogó's friend talked a lot; he talked about the Sudan, about Zimbabwe, Kenya and Nigeria, he talked about the Masai, the Batusi and the Zulus, and also about the chief of an Ethiopian tribe, whose name was Abebe-Aba-ba-Abebe. And after talking about all these things, he talked about the jungle and about lions.

"The lion is a magnificent beast," said the friend. "He's strong, powerful and noble. He's the King of the Jungle. There's no animal he can't vanquish. He can strike a hunter dead with the last beat of his heart."

Shola, who had been dozing in the armchair, pricked up her ears. What sort of beast
was this lion, so like herself in so many ways?
She too was strong, powerful and noble.
Although she had never actually fought with
anyone or seen a hunter, she was sure that

they would all be afraid of her; she was sure that all animals and all hunters were aware—painfully aware—that she could strike them dead with the last beat of her heart.

"So..." Shola wagged her tail doubtfully, "if I'm a lion, why does Grogó insist on calling me a mere mutt?"

Shola was in the grip of these terrible doubts when the friend brought his visit to an end.

"I'll take you home," said Señor Grogó. "I fancy a walk. Are you coming, Shola?"

"Not me," said she. "I don't feel like going out. I've got a lot of things to think about."

When she was alone, Shola noticed that Grogó's friend had left a book on the chair, and she craned her neck to read the title. Her heart turned over, and that was because of what was on the cover, and what was on the cover was this: *The Lion, King of the Jungle*.

This was just what she needed if she was to find out whether she really was just a mutt or whether she was, in fact, a lion. Shola opened the book at the first page and started reading, and what she read was this:

The lion is a strong, powerful and noble animal, feared by all. He is the undisputed king of the jungle.

"So everyone agrees, then," thought Shola, remembering what Grogó's friend had said. "I must study this book properly."

She picked up the book and carried it off to her hidey hole, the place where she kept her bones and her toys. Then she returned and lay down on the armchair, where she remained until Señor Grogó came back.

"Shola," said Grogó as soon as he came in the room, "have you seen a book lying around? My friend left it in here somewhere."

"I haven't seen anything," she said.

"Are you sure?" insisted Grogó, who knew what a liar she was.

"Powerful, noble creatures like myself never lie," declared Shola, who was already feeling a little like a lioness.

From that day on, Shola showed very little

interest in going for walks. She said she no longer wanted to do what she had always done, and that she preferred staying at home. Señor Grogó shrugged his shoulders and went out by himself.

"What are you playing at, Shola?" he asked after she had gone three whole days without once wanting to go out for a walk.

"I'm not *playing* at anything," replied Shola.

But she was playing at something. By that time, Shola was convinced, utterly convinced, that she was a lioness. It wasn't just *her* opinion, the book confirmed it:

These powerful animals are very lazy.
They spend most of the day lying down,
in the shade if possible, and they only get
up in order to go in search of food.

"It all fits," thought Shola when she read this. "Besides, I have always been a rather unusual dog. My mother used to say as much. 'No one would think you were a daughter of mine, Shola,' she would say, 'I'm really tidy, while you, on the other hand, don't know the meaning of the word!'"

Now it could all be explained. She couldn't be her mother's daughter, she couldn't be a tidy little dog. She couldn't, because she wasn't a dog. She was a lion or, rather, a lioness, which amounted to the same thing.

Señor Grogó soon noticed these changes in Shola's behaviour. It wasn't just that she refused to go out for walks, it was the slow, slow way she walked, the way she held her head up all the time, as if she had a crick in her neck, and the way she barked, if you could call it barking, since the sounds Shola made were more like toots on a rather squeaky toy trumpet.

Señor Grogó decided that he would have to be firm. He would take her out for a walk whether she wanted to go or not. Of course, why not, I mean, honestly, enough was enough, he had to put an end to this bizarre behaviour.

"We're going for a walk in the park, Shola! And I won't take no for an answer!"

"I didn't say no," said Shola cheekily. "I want to go for a walk in the jungle."

"Why do you call the park the jungle?"
asked Grogó.

"That's what all my family call it. As if
you didn't know."

"Well no, actually, I didn't," said Grogó
bemused.

"Well, now you do," declared Shola, head-
ing for the door with that slow, slow gait of
hers, with her head up as if she had a crick
in her neck.

As soon as they got to the jungle, I mean, park, Shola wanted to find out whether or not it was true that all the animals were afraid of her. She looked around her. Nothing, only a little boy over there, three retired gentlemen in one corner, and in the other corner... in the other corner was something to hunt—a flock of pigeons was fluttering around in front of a little old lady scattering breadcrumbs. Before Grogó could stop her, Shola was racing towards them.

A moment later, the startled pigeons were flying off and the little old lady was

screaming. Shola again made that noise like someone blowing triumphantly on a squeaky toy trumpet. Señor Grogó had to apologize to the little old lady.

"I'm so sorry, madam, I don't know what's got into her. She's been acting very strangely lately. She's never attacked any pigeons before."

"She's a wild beast," the little old lady was shouting, "that's what she is, a wild beast!"

"Thank you, madam," said Shola contentedly. She *was* a wild beast, a wild beast from the jungle, in fact. And she felt so happy that she didn't even notice the scolding Señor

Grogó gave her. In fact, she felt very happy indeed.

She felt happier still when a duck in the park told her off for what she had done to the little old lady and the pigeons.

"That was really nasty of you. The park is meant for everyone, but especially for us ducks, because altogether there are more than two hundred ducks here."

"Clear off, you stupid duck," said Shola very arrogantly. "If you don't, I will strike you dead with the last beat of my heart!"

"What do you think you are, a lion?" asked the duck impertinently.

"Take a good look at me!" said Shola.

"I am looking at you," said the duck, "and all I see is a little white dog. And as far as I know, lions are definitely not white."

Having said that, the duck strolled off with the same gait that Shola had been using ever since she read the book on lions—with his head up, as if he had a crick in his neck, and walking very, very slowly.

Shola watched him move off. She felt worried. Was it true that lions weren't white?

"I'll have to look it up in the book," she thought.

Unfortunately, the book agreed with the duck.

The skin of the lion is a beautiful golden brown, like the colour of fire.

That was what it said. There was no mention of any exceptions.

Shola thought long and hard. She belonged to the family of lions, she was sure of that, because everything that she had read up until then confirmed it, but why had she changed colour? There must be a reason, there must be.

"There must be," she said to herself. "I must have been golden once."

"Yes, now I remember," she said to herself a while later. "When I was little, I was definitely golden."

"Yes," she said to herself some hours later still. "I remember it well, yes, I remember it perfectly. When I was a few months old, I was golden, very golden. My fur was a very beautiful colour, the colour of fire. Everyone used to tell me what lovely fur I had. I don't know how I could have forgotten that."

"Yes," she thought at last, "it's all coming back. I used to be golden and then, with the passing of time, I've become what I am now, a white lion. The same thing happened with one of our neighbours; his hair used to be blond and now it's white."

After these arduous reflections, Shola ran to the bathroom and started rummaging around in the cabinet. After a lot of rummaging, she found what she was looking for—a little bottle containing a liquid used for dyeing hair blond. Shola poured it all over her back.

When Grogó saw her, he stood there open-mouthed.

"Shola, what have you done to your fur?"

"I've restored it to its original colour," replied Shola, not deigning even to look at him.

"Its original colour? But you've always been a little white dog."

"Don't call me a dog, I'm not a dog. You're quite mistaken."

"What are you then?" exclaimed Grogó, astonished.

"I belong to the family of lions."

"Lions? But lions live in the jungle!"

"That's where I come from actually."

And with that, Shola left the room, walking very, very slowly. On her way down the corridor, she looked at herself in the mirror, pulled a fierce face and yelled: "I can strike a man dead with the last beat of my heart!"

She followed these fierce words with the roar that sounded like someone blowing on a squeaky toy trumpet.

Grogó had seen the whole thing and felt very worried. What was going on? He didn't know, but just in case he was going to keep a close eye on her when he took her to the park. Shola was capable of anything.

"Time will tell," he thought.

And time did tell, and this is what happened.

Shola had gone on reading the book about lions because she was eager to remember what she had been like before she had been deceived into thinking that she was a mere dog, a mutt. She was almost at the end of the book when she read the following words:

Lions hate captivity and consider it undignified to receive food from human hands. Any lion worthy of the name goes out hunting for his own food.

Shola nodded again and again, yes, yes, that was absolutely right, she remembered it well. She remembered clearly how, when she was very little, she would refuse to eat from the plate that Grogó set before her. Then Grogó had made her eat, and she had gradually got used to it. That's how it had all happened.

"Not any more!" said Shola firmly. "I will never again accept anything from a human hand!"

As soon as Señor Grogó came home, she told him of her decision.

"I'm going out hunting, I'm hungry."

"You're hungry?" said Grogó. "Well, if you wait a bit, Shola, I'm just about to make your supper."

"What's for supper, then?" asked Shola, pausing at the door.

"Mince," said Grogó.

Shola hesitated; she hesitated for a long time. She had the feeling that she could already smell the mince, and her mouth began to water.

"I can't give in, a true lion wouldn't!" she thought, and she gritted her teeth and tried to forget the smell of mince, the treacherous smell that you could smell even before it reached you. At last she said:

"I consider it beneath me to receive food from the hands of humans. I'm going out to hunt. From time to time, I will return to visit you."

Before Grogó could respond, Shola had gone down the stairs and out of the apartment. Soon afterwards, she was back in the jungle, I mean, in the park near the apartment.

"Right, let's get hunting!" she said to herself.

Saying that was one thing; however, doing it was quite another. Between thought and act there's quite a gap, and that gap, in Shola's

case, seemed very large. There was no one to be seen in the park. Not a duck, not a little old lady, not even a wretched pigeon. The night had scared them all away.

"The jungle's awfully lonely," she thought sadly.

At that moment her stomach made a little noise, a sort of *grrup*. It was a very small grrup, barely noticeable, but enough to alarm her. There was no doubt about it, that noise meant that her stomach was empty.

"I'd better try another jungle," she said after a while. The truth was that she felt a bit afraid of leaving that jungle or park or whatever it was, but she had no option. She had to go off into the unknown.

"Besides," she said, to give herself courage, "being who I am, powerful and strong, I shouldn't be afraid of anything."

Feeling calmer, she began to walk along one of the avenues in the city, past bright neon signs and rubbish bins, past traffic lights and sleeping cars.

She had been walking for a while when she spotted a cat.

"A cat!" she shouted. "Tally-ho!"

And giving that squeaky toy trumpet roar, Shola raced off towards her prey.

However, something very odd happened. The cat, which from a distance had looked like a little tiny kitten, close up turned out to be a great huge tomcat. This great huge tomcat was rummaging around in a rubbish bin, and didn't even turn a hair when, from a matter of yards away, Shola gave her little toy trumpet roar.

"It really is an enormous cat," thought Shola, not daring to move any closer. "And as well as being enormous, it's also very strange. It's as if it were deaf. Yes, it must be deaf. Otherwise it would have run away as soon as it heard me roaring."

Of course, it must be deaf. Not only did it not run away, it ignored Shola completely.

"I hope, at least, it isn't blind," said Shola to herself as she bounded up to the cat.

The cat was not in fact blind. At last he deigned to notice Shola.

"Look, titch," he said to her. "This rubbish bin is mine, so just tootle on off."

Shola was about to inform him that she could strike him dead with the last beat of her heart, but she decided to keep quiet instead.

In fact, the enormous tomcat was quite right: that *was* his rubbish bin. Why argue? After all, wasn't it more important that animals should live in harmony together? Cats and lions, for example? Yes, that was much more important. Besides, that cat really was very large, huge in fact.

"Listen," said Shola at last, "do you know of any jungles around here?"

"Well, you could try Burma," said the cat with *purr*fect aplomb.

"Right, I will, thank you," said Shola. She had no idea where on the map Burma might

be, but continuing her conversation with the cat didn't seem like a good idea either.

Suddenly, her stomach said grrup grrup, slightly louder than before.

"I'm not behaving like a true lion," said Shola. "The fact is that my stomach is very, very empty, and I still haven't found any food."

Her stomach agreed with her, uttering a long grrruuuupp.

Shola walked and walked until she reached a square. It was empty, no cats, no little old ladies, no pigeons, nothing. Well, there was something, a rubbish bin with half its contents spilled on the ground.

"I'll go and see if there are any scraps to eat."

Rummaging around for scraps didn't seem quite appropriate for a member of the lion family. The book didn't say anything about lions eating that kind of thing. Of course, it didn't say they didn't either. Besides, her stomach was making more and more noise.

"I'm *so* hungry," she exclaimed, when she was already standing next to the rubbish bin.

But the bin smelled awful. It stank of cigarettes and rotting food and withered, forgotten flowers.

"I can't eat this! I just can't," howled Shola. She almost felt like crying. She couldn't bear the smell. And the worst thing was that it reminded her, by contrast, of the smell of

mince, fried mince with a little salt, mince
mixed with bits of bone, mince, mince, mince.
Her mouth began to water.

Shola sat down on a bench in the square
and set to thinking. While she was doing that,
her stomach began its customary grrup grrup.

"The truth is I'm not very powerful," she
said to herself humbly. "I'm not very strong
or very noble either. In fact, I'm very small
and a terrible liar."

Her stomach gave three grrups one after
the other.

"I'm so hungry," she said. "And I'm a complete liar. I can't *really* remember having once been golden. I've never been golden. I've always been white. I don't know why I tell myself such lies."

At that moment, her stomach filled with noises. It was no longer a solitary grrup, now it was more like a bombardment—grrup, blatz, sshiip, grrummm, groummm. Shola realized that she could bear it no longer. She looked at the solitary square, she looked at the solitary dustbin, she looked up at the solitary stars and she cried out:

"I'm not a lioness! I'm just a little dog! You can keep your lions!"

Shola set off at a run. She crossed the square, ran down the avenue, plunged into the

jungle, I mean, the park, went up the stairs of her apartment and scratched at Grogó's door with her paws.

"So our lioness is back!" smiled Grogó mockingly.

"I made a mistake," said Shola by way of an excuse. "What's wrong with that? Don't you ever make mistakes?"

"Of course I do," said Grogó.

"Yes, you're *always* making mistakes. I, on the other hand, very rarely make mistakes. But that's life."

"It would be nice if, just once, Shola, you could be a little less cheeky and arrogant."

Señor Grogó shouted and complained, but Shola couldn't hear him. She had already

gone into the kitchen, where she was gobbling down as fast as she could the mince that had been prepared for her a few hours earlier, when she still belonged to the very noble, very powerful family of lions.

BERNARDO ATXAGA

Bernardo Atxaga is the author of several books, including *Two Brothers*, *Obabakoak* (Euskadi Prize, Spanish National Award for Narrative, finalist for the IMPAC European Literary Award), *The Lone Man*, *The Lone Woman*, *The Accordionist's Son* (Grinzane Cavour Award, Mondello Prize, *Times Literary Supplement* Translation Prize) and *Seven Houses in France* (longlisted for the *Independent* Foreign Fiction Prize; one of the best fiction books published in 2012 in USA, according to *Publishers Weekly*). His books have been translated into thirty-two languages.

MIKEL VALVERDE

Born in Vitoria-Gasteiz, the prize-winning writer and illustrator Mikel Valverde studied at the Fine Arts Faculty of the Basque Public University, where he started creating comics, and illustrations for his own stories. One day he met Bernardo Atxaga in the neighbourhood where they both lived, and so began both their friendship and their working relationship. They have published several books together since then, in addition to the Shola stories.

MARGARET JULL COSTA

Margaret Jull Costa has been a literary translator for nearly thirty years, and has translated works by Portuguese, Spanish and Latin American writers – among them Bernardo Atxaga, Eça de Queiroz, Javier Marías and José Saramago.

PUSHKIN CHILDREN'S BOOKS

Just as we all are, children are fascinated by stories. From the earliest age, we love to hear about monsters and heroes, romance and death, disaster and rescue, from every place and time.

We created Pushkin Children's Books to share these tales from different languages and cultures with younger readers, and to open the door to the wide, colourful worlds these stories offer.

From picture books and adventure stories to fairy tales and classics, and from fifty-year-old bestsellers to current huge successes abroad, the books on the Pushkin Children's list reflect the very best stories from around the world, for our most discerning readers of all: children.

THE WITCH IN THE BROOM CUPBOARD
AND OTHER TALES

PIERRE GRIPARI

Illustrated by Fernando Puig Rosado

'Wonderful... funny, tender and daft'
David Almond

THE STORY OF THE BLUE PLANET

ANDRI SNÆR MAGNASON

Illustrated by Áslaug Jónsdóttir

'A Seussian mix of wonder, wit and gravitas'
The New York Times

SHOLA AND THE LIONS

BERNARDO ATXAGA

Illustrated by Mikel Valverde

'Gently ironic stories... totally charming'
Independent

THE POINTLESS LEOPARD:
WHAT GOOD ARE KIDS ANYWAY?

COLAS GUTMAN

Illustrated by Delphine Perret

'Lively, idiomatic and always entertaining...
a decidedly offbeat little book'
Robert Dunbar, *Irish Times*

POCKETY: THE TORTOISE WHO LIVED AS SHE PLEASED

FLORENCE SEYVOS

Illustrated by Claude Ponti

'A treasure – a real find – and one of the most enjoyable
children's books I've read in a while... This is a tortoise
that deserves to win every literary race'
Observer

THE LETTER FOR THE KING

TONKE DRAGT

'Gripping from its opening moment onwards, this
award-winning book doesn't miss a beat from its
thrilling beginning to its satisfying ending'
Julia Eccleshare

THE PILOT AND THE LITTLE PRINCE

PETER SÍS

'With its extraordinary, sophisticated illustrations,
its poetry and the historical detail of the text, this
book will reward readers of any age over eight'
Sunday Times

SAVE THE STORY

GULLIVER · ANTIGONE · CAPTAIN NEMO · DON JUAN
GILGAMESH · THE BETROTHED · THE NOSE
CYRANO DE BERGERAC · KING LEAR · CRIME AND PUNISHMENT

'An amazing new series from Pushkin Press in which
literary, adult authors retell classics (with terrific
illustrations) for a younger generation'
Daily Telegraph

THE CAT WHO CAME IN OFF THE ROOF
ANNIE M.G. SCHMIDT

'Guaranteed to make anyone 7-plus to 107 who likes to
curl up with a book and a cat purr with pleasure'
The Times

THE OKSA POLLOCK SERIES
ANNE PLICHOTA AND CENDRINE WOLF

Part 1 · *The Last Hope*

Part 2 · *The Forest of Lost Souls*

Part 3 · *The Heart of Two Worlds*

'A feisty heroine, lots of sparky tricks and evil opponents
could fill a gap left by the end of the Harry Potter series'
Daily Mail

THE VITELLO SERIES
KIM FUPZ AAKESON

Illustrated by Niels Bo Bojesen

'Full of quirky humour and an anarchic sense
of fun that children will love'
Booktrust

A HOUSE WITHOUT MIRRORS
MÅRTEN SANDÉN

Illustrated by Moa Schulman

'A classic story that has it all'
Dagens Nyheter